WHERE IS THE
Pastor?
WHERE IS OUR
Shepherd?

Lillian Scott

authorHOUSE®

AuthorHouse™
1663 Liberty Drive
Bloomington, IN 47403
www.authorhouse.com
Phone: 1 (800) 839-8640

Published by AuthorHouse 07/17/2017

ISBN: 978-1-5462-0013-0 (sc)
ISBN: 978-1-5462-0012-3 (e)

Print information available on the last page.

Any people depicted in stock imagery provided by Thinkstock are models,
and such images are being used for illustrative purposes only.
Certain stock imagery © Thinkstock.

This book is printed on acid-free paper.

Because of the dynamic nature of the Internet, any web addresses or links contained in
this book may have changed since publication and may no longer be valid. The views
expressed in this work are solely those of the author and do not necessarily reflect the
views of the publisher, and the publisher hereby disclaims any responsibility for them.

DEDICATION

First, I thank God for letting the words come to me freely.

I would like to dedicate this book to my husband of thirty-seven years, Joe Lewis. He came into my life during a difficult time. He always stands by me and supports me in whatever I do. I could not have accomplished the many things I have done without him. I am happy God put him in my life.

To my beautiful grandchildren Malik and Chynna, I love you and am so very proud of you.

To my wonderful family and supportive friends, thank you.

I would like to thank my dear friend Sister Renee Brascomb for her encouragement and for giving me the inspiration to write this book.

Thank you to all women both young and not so young. You can overcome any obstacles.

It has been a joy for me to express my feelings on these pages.

I can do all things through Christ which strengtheneth me (Philippians 4:13).

CONTENTS

PROLOGUE

This story begins one year ago. The church service was just beginning on that Sunday morning. There was a light dusting of snow on the ground. Members were very slowly ushered in by the head usher Sister Missy Starr. She was always at her post. Had Sister Lucinda Smith remembered to do the mass call to let the members know the service would start later due to the weather?

The praise and worship team of ten people were singing their hearts out. Mother Hatfield joined in with her favorite song—whatever her favorite song of the day was.

Everyone was getting into the service, when all of a sudden, there was a loud, thunderous crash! The entire choir platform with the musicians and equipment crashed into the basement. Everyone was yelling and praying. They asked, "Where is the pastor? Where is our shepherd?"

CHAPTER 1

The Beginning

In 1929, John Lee Hatfield was born in the hills of West Virginia. John was the apple of his parents' eyes. He was a smart child, who was always willing to learn.

His parents worked in the coal mines. His father was a miner and his mother worked in the office. Little John was not afraid of work. He helped his parents in the coal mines after school. He worked in the family's massive vegetable garden on the weekends. He loved to please his parents.

Later, his parents had eight more children. John had four brothers and four sisters. He had little time for school, because he had to help take care of his brothers and sisters and work. He vowed that when he had his own children, they would all complete high school and go to college.

As the years passed, John would go into town with his parents' permission to sell vegetables they had grown. On one of those trips he met the love of his life, Miss Mattie Love. That day, she was with her parents, Carl and Connie Love.

She worked at C&C, the local dry cleaners, which was owned by her parents. John was sweet on her.

She was from the other side of town. Her parents owned a home in town. She even had a car for transportation. Mattie Love was the only child of Carl and Connie Love. She was tall and slender like her dad. When she smiled, you could see her dimples. She wore her hair in a long pageboy. She always wore high heels and a fashionable blazer with a matching skirt.

John started taking his work clothes into the cleaners where Miss Mattie worked. This went on for several months until he got the nerve to ask her for a date. He was very shy. Miss Mattie told young John he had to ask her father before she could accept. Miss Mattie invited him to her parents' home for Sunday dinner.

Mr. Carl Love was a tall slender man and a very stern father and husband. He protected his family. Many evenings, you would find him in his recliner, smoking his pipe and listening to the radio.

Mattie's mother, Connie Love, was a frail God-fearing woman. She was involved in many ministries at her church. This is what she enjoyed most. She did not work outside of the home. On rare occasions, she would come into the dry cleaners to visit with Mattie.

John asked Mr. Love if he could take Miss Mattie on a date. Mr. Love gave his permission, but he had to know where they were going, and she had to be home at 9 p.m.—not a minute after. Their first date was at the ice cream parlor. They dated for several months.

Miss Mattie was a Christian. She went to Mount Sebastian Church with her parents every Sunday. She sang in the choir and played the piano. She invited John to join her and her family at church. At first John was a little leery. He figured the only way he could see more of Miss Mattie was to go to church, so he did.

John eventually joined the church and began playing the guitar at services. He formed a group that began to perform at other churches in the area.

John asked Mr. Love for Miss Mattie's hand in marriage after several years of courting. They eventually married. The wedding was huge, the talk of the town. The town had gotten to know John through his music, and they knew Miss Mattie as the only child of Carl and Connie Love, and working in the family dry cleaning business.

After marrying, they discussed moving up north where John would have more opportunities. Miss Mattie was torn. She hated to leave her parents and the town she loved, but she knew she should be by her husband's side. So they migrated north.

They settled in the small town of Seaside, New Jersey, named for its location on the shore. Miss Mattie worked for a short time at the local cleaners, as she had in her hometown. She made friends with the local residents. She joined the local church, Northernlite.

John worked in construction at the local yacht club. This experience would be valuable to him in the future. He took many of the influential and wealthy residents on yachting and fishing trips. Members of the yacht club always asked for John because he had such a kind and gentle manner about him. John worked many long hours.

Sometimes, Mattie would accompany him. At times she would prepare a nice buffet for him and the passengers. They were both hard workers. They saved their money so they would be able to buy a home one day. The Hatfields were ready to start a family of their own.

CHAPTER 2

Our Family

John and Mattie Hatfield worked for seven long and prosperous years, John at the yacht club and Mattie at the cleaners. At times she also worked with her husband on the yacht. He chartered tours along the shore line to New York City. Mattie, who was an excellent cook, would prepare huge buffets on board as part of the tour package. She had made friends with the local women in town, and as friends told other friends about their little business, it grew tremendously.

Eventually, John was able to buy a small yacht, and the couple were able to buy a home to begin their long-awaited family. Mattie wanted many children to love. As an only child, she had always felt alone. John wanted what Mattie wanted. She was the love of his life.

One hot summer evening on the yacht, Mattie told her husband she was pregnant. They were both thrilled. On Valentine's Day, Mattie gave birth to identical twin boys, Joseph and Jeremy. The boys were the best of both of them. They would take their sons out on the yacht every chance they could. They taught them how to swim and fish. Mattie stopped working at the cleaners. She concentrated on her family.

Two years later, God blessed John and Mattie with twin girls on Christmas Day. They named the girls Faith and Holly. Their growing family continued to work on their yacht. The boys adored their little sisters. They enjoyed these times together.

Mattie took her little family to church every Sunday. John spent his Sundays on the yacht. Mattie kept praying John would go to church with her and the children.

Another blessing came two years later. Mattie was pregnant again. She gave birth to another set of twin girls. She named them Marci and Mindy.

The family moved into a larger home to accommodate their growing family. Mattie's mother came to help her with their six small children.

Mattie wondered why she had had three sets of twins. When she asked her mother if twins ran in their family. Mattie's mom told her a long-kept secret: Mattie herself was a twin. Her twin, however, had died at birth, and Mattie's mother had gone into a deep depression. She had not been able to function for many years. Mattie's father had taken on most of the household responsibilities until his wife was able to. Now Mattie knew why she had always felt alone—there really was an absence in her life.

Mattie enjoyed her family. John occasionally began to go to church with them.

Three years later, Mattie had yet another set of twins, Johnathan and Jessie. Matties doctor told Mattie it was extremely rare for a woman to have four sets of twins. Mattie felt this was a true blessing from God. Mattie kept busy with her eight children, John, the yacht tours, and her home. The family enjoyed the water and their time on the yacht. When Joseph and Jeremy were ten, and Holly and Faith were eight, they were able to help their parents on weekends with the yacht tours. The four younger children stayed home with their auntie, John's elder sister Carrie. She had come from West Virginia to help her brother and sister-in-law with the children. Her four children were grown. She had recently been widowed after forty years of marriage. She had plenty of time on her hands. She enjoyed the shore and decided to stay.

Mattie felt her life was almost complete. She kept praying John would give his life to Christ and that he would go to church with his family more.

CHAPTER 3

Prayer Answered

John and Mattie were happy and thriving. The children were teenagers now. They were busy with sports, dance recitals, and church functions. On the weekends, the children were able to help their parents on the yacht. They were involved in the community, giving their time to the food bank and volunteering at the hospital and nursing home. The children were a great joy to their parents.

The girls sang in the church choir. The boys played instruments at church. They were known as the Hatfield twins. Four sets of twins in one family was a blessing. They were well-known in their community.

Mattie's prayers were finally answered. John accepted Christ. He was baptized on Easter Sunday morning in the presence of his wife, children, and congregation.

Over the years, the family kept busy with their many activities. Joseph and Jeremy were looking into colleges. John was prepared for his children to attend college. This was something he believed in. He was not able to go to college, but he was determined to to send his children if they wanted to go. Joseph and Jeremy were accepted into Hampton University in Virginia. They wanted to be together. They were never apart.

The other children were sad their brothers were going away for the first time without them. As they continued to help their parents on the yacht during the summers and with their community activities and church functions, they knew they would one day go to college too.

Joseph and Jeremy excelled in college. They enjoyed their experience. They were on the Dean's List. They played basketball and hockey. Joseph was on the chess team. Jeremy was on the debate team.

Now it was time for Holly and Faith to go to college. The girls decided to go to separate colleges. They wanted to experience being apart for the first time. Holly chose New York University to study law. Faith decided to go to Brown University in Rhode Island to study public administration and social services.

Four children were in college. The house was much quieter with four children gone. John and Mattie kept busy with their many obligations.

John went to church on a regular basis. God was using him. John was ordained as a deacon. He would serve as a deacon for several years.

Then God called John to preach. He told Mattie that God had called him to preach. Mattie's prayers were answered. John served as assistant pastor at the Ocean by the Sea Church until God told him it was time to move. Then he was ready to pastor his own church.

Joseph and Jeremy had graduated from college. They were doing well in their careers. Joseph was a biology teacher, and Jeremy was a math teacher. They loved teaching. They would visit their family when possible and spend their summers with their parents, as they missed being on the water.

John was in the process of building his church. The four younger children were helping their parents. Their church was now Mount Grace. Mount Grace was a small, white-framed church on a hill. The stained-glass windows were beautiful. There was a cross in the center of each window.

The church overlooked the small shore town. There would be room for expansion as their membership grew.

The Hatfield family marched into the new church on November 20, 1979. By then, Holly and Faith had graduated from college and were able to attend with their family. Holly was an attorney in New York City, and Faith was a social worker in Connecticut.

CHAPTER 4

Mount Grace

Reverend John Hatfield was a dramatic preacher. He led many people to Christ. As first lady, Sister Mattie was so proud. She stood by her husband's side.

Marci and Mindy were in their third year at college. Marci at Monmouth University and Mindy at Kean. The girls wanted to stay close to home. They missed the shore. They missed their parents.

Johnathan and Jessie decided that college was not for them. They wanted to serve their country. They went into the military. Johnathan went into the marines, and Jessie went into the navy. Their parents were so proud of their sons' choice to serve.

Mount Grace Church continued to grow under the leadership of Reverend Hatfield. Reverend Hatfiel traveled to many churches in New Jersey, Philadelphia, New York, and Connecticut to preach. The congregation traveled with him for support.

Reverend Hatfield took Timothy DoLittle under his wing as his young assistant pastor. Brother Timothy DoLittle first had become a trustee. After much studying, he was ordained as a deacon. Deacon DoLittle traveled with Reverend Hatfield. God called him to preach after several years of studying under Reverend Hatfield. Pastor Timothy DoLittle was ordained and became Reverend Hatfield's right-hand man.

The church continued to grow. Many souls were saved. many new members joined, and many children were baptized.

The Sunday school grew as well. Sister Nora Lane, who had been a Sunday school teacher for fifty years, was now superintendent at Mount Grace. She loved children. Until her retirement ten years earlier, she had been a kindergarten teacher at the elementary school, and she still volunteered occasionally at Head Start.

Sister Lane and her assistant Sister Joyce Day were kept busy with the children. When Sister Lane was away, Sister Day took over her responsibilities and was glad she could be of service. Sister Lane spent a month in Soweto, South Africa, setting up Sunday school classes with the missionaries. The little children were anxious to learn about God. Her next trip would be to an orphanage in Labadee, Haiti.

Nora Lane had been married for sixty years to Carlton. Her husband was now confined to a wheelchair. Nurse Jayleen Grumble would arrange his care while Nora was away.

God's work kept Reverend Hatfield and First Lady Mattie Hatfield quite busy. They no longer had time for the yacht. Marci and Mindy would take the yacht out for tours to help their parents.

Reverend Hatfield's revivals were famous all over the state. Many souls were saved. Mount Grace was full every Sunday morning. Seats had to be put in the aisles for the overflow. Reverend Timothy DoLittle assisted Reverend Hatfield. Many deacons and trustees were ordained.

Sister Hatfield was busy working in the church along with her husband. She organized fish fries, fed the poor, and visited nursing home patients. If you were hungry, you could always find a meal at her home.

She had all she had prayed for. Her children were all saved and doing well. Her older twins, Joseph and Jeremy, were married to women she adored. She and Reverend Hatfield were about to become grandparents.

Justice Ritz began coming to Mount Grace after his children joined. He was a retired Navy SEAL. His family had recently relocated to the area. His children were baptized by Reverend Hatfield and sang in the choir. Brother Ritz joined Mount Grace. He helped Reverend Hatfield with financial matters and became a trustee. Then God called Brother Ritz to preach. He was ordained by Reverend Hatfield and became an assistant pastor. Reverend Ritz taught classes for new members and Bible studies, and led prayer services.

CHAPTER 5

Deacon and Deaconess

Mount Grace continued to grow over the years. Many new members joined during this time. Deacon and Deaconess Clay were among the new members. The Clays had sold their home in Arkansas and had come to New Jersey several years earlier. They had been looking for a church home. After much prayer, God led them to Mount Grace.

They had worked diligently and had served God with their children. Their children were now grown, and they felt alone. Their children had families of their own and had relocated to California and Texas.

Deaconess Clay loved to cook and clean. She held fish fries to raise money to support the church. She also held yard and garage sales to support Mount Grace.

The pastor needed a president for the Pastor's Aid Ministry. Deaconess Clara Clay volunteered. Her retirement from the civil defense department gave her time to help the church as much as possible. Her husband had retired from Amtrak, though he still worked part-time as an Uber driver.

Deaconess Clay had plenty of time on her hands and stepped right in. She became the president of the Pastor's Aid Ministry, but she needed some help to carry out her duties. She prayed that the right person would come along to help her.

Soon she met Deaconess Jean Green. They had the same interests. God had answered her prayers. Deaconess Jean Green became her assistant.

Deaconess Green had retired after working for thirty years as supervisor in the janitorial department at the local hospital. She had enjoyed her position as supervisor and had trained many young people to do a thorough job.

The two women worked well together. They both loved to clean, cook, and eat. They sponsored yearly banquets, afternoon services, and dinners. They seemed tireless. Many hours were devoted to help Reverend and First Lady Hatfield and their family. Sometimes, they would ask Sister Weeks, the choir director, and her daughter Exxon to help. They worked well together.

But Deaconess Green was feeling at a loss. Her only son and his family had just moved to Florida. Her husband was still working as a used car salesman and auto mechanic. He was much younger than she was, but the age difference didn't matter to them. She knew he was a God-fearing man. They had met at church. They became instant friends first, and then they married. It did not upset them at all that she was known as a cougar around town. They knew their love was true. God had joined them together. They had one son and two lovely grandchildren.

One day, Deaconess Green had just finished six donuts when she found herself becoming faint. A week earlier, she had had an episode and had to go to the ER. It turned out that she was a diabetic.

"Let's pray for strength," Deaconess Clay said. She thought some fresh air would be good for Deaconess Green.

"Let's go to Reverend Hatfield's house to do our weekly house cleaning," Deaconess Green insisted.

While they were cleaning Reverend Hatfield's house, Deaconess Green took a break to go into the kitchen to get bottles of water for them. It was an extremely hot day.

"Our next step is to clean the chandeliers," she said. "But first let's turn on the TV to see what is going on in the world."

Suddenly a late-breaking news report came on. Major Johnathan Hatfield of the US Marines was missing and presumed to be captured in an undisclosed location. The women recognized Johnathan as one of the youngest sons of Reverend and First Lady Hatfield.

"Oh my God," they both screamed and started praying for his safety.

CHAPTER 6

Missing

The Hatfields customarily held the church's annual picnic at their home, a gorgeous six-bedroom house, white with green trim, on the hill overlooking the bay and golf course. Surrounding it were beautiful gardens that provided vegetables and flowers for the gathering.

First Lady Hatfield loved her flowers. She wanted always to see and smell her flowers. Fresh flowers were everywhere.

The picnic was always the highlight of the season. The entire church was invited, and no one turned down this invitation. First Lady Hatfield still did a lot of the cooking, as she had those many years ago for the yacht tours, but now with a little help from the Pastor's Aid Ministry.

The Hatfields had bought this home at a bargain price through the many contacts they had made in their yacht business. They still kept in touch with the friends they had made during those years, and they could always call on a favor, if needed.

All of their children had grown up in this home. They enjoyed summers with their grandchildren when they came to visit. First Lady Hatfield was glad God had blessed her with such a family.

This was the beautiful home that Deaconess Clara Clay and Deaconess Jean Green loved cleaning. They were in their own dreamworld. And God was good.

But now Major Johnathan Hatfield was missing. Johnathan Hatfield had made a career in the service. He had gone to college in the service. He became a second lieutenant and then, advanced to first lieutenant. Lieutenant Hatfield had saved his squad during a major battle. He was promoted to captain. He received the Purple Heart and was promoted to major.

Major Hatfield loved the military and made it his life's career. He had not married. The marines had been his life.

The entire congregation at Mount Grace was proud of him, especially his parents. When he came home on leave, he always visited Mount Grace. He spent time with the young men and discussed the rewards of military life. He was a role model in the community.

Jessie Hatfield was following in his twin brothers footsteps. He was making a career in the military. He enlisted in the Navy. He completed college in the service. The Navy gave him a chance to be on the sea. This reminded him of his days on the yacht with his family. Johnathan and Jessie were always in competition with each other.

Jessie moved up through the ranks. He was a seaman, and then Ensign Hatfield was promoted to Lieutenant Junior. After eleven years Lieutenant Hatfield was promoted to captain.

Captain Jessie Hatfield was loyal to the Navy and his men. Captain Jessie Hatfield continued his dedication to the Navy. He was now in charge of the Navy fleet of aircraft carriers in the Arabian Gulf. He was now in his element as the carriers crossed vast stretches of ocean.

Jessie was given leave when the news reached him his brother was missing to be with his family. They prayed together to bring Johnathan home.

News spreads so fast through the community and churches. When Reverend Hatfield heard the news, he collapsed in the pulpit and was rushed to the emergency room. It was a massive heart attack. He was admitted to ICU. First Lady Hatfield remained by his side in the hospital.

When the story broke that Major Hatfield was missing, Victoria Fox, the youngest daughter of Sister Lucinda Smith, was doing her summer internship under the senior reporter at the local paper. Victoria had grown up with the younger Hatfield children. They had gone to school and church together, and she had sung in the choir with them.

Victoria and her sister, Veronica, had spent many hours on their yacht. She had been close to Johnathan Hatfield and always called him Jon. At one time, Victoria had considered the military as a career. Now she felt she could be of more service reporting on the men and women who served their country. She prayed for the family and the release of Jon.

Head nurse Jayleen Grumble was in charge of Reverend Hatfield's care. She was a compassionate woman of God and an excellent nurse. Reverend Hatfield received wonderful care under her watch.

Nurse Grumble was a personal friend of Sister Lucinda Smith. She had worshipped at Mount Grace often with her children. Nurse Grumble and her children had joined Mount Grace and she had become the nurse on duty there.

Reverend Hatfield remained in ICU for several days. He gradually improved, but he remained weak. He was not able to preach for many Sundays. Reverend Timothy DoLittle and Reverend Justice Ritz conducted services for him.

Reverend Justice Ritz, the retired Navy SEAL, was a tall, distinguished, elderly man. He carried himself as he if he were still in the military. He had made his career in the service. He was a widower, and many of the sisters were interested in him, but his focus was on God and God only.

Reverend Ritz delivered powerful sermons on the first Sunday of each month, when he was in charge of communion. He also led the prayer services on Wednesday afternoons and taught Bible study on Thursday evenings. He was such an excellent teacher, that his classes were in high demand.

Reverend Timothy DoLittle was recently divorced from his second wife. No one ever mentioned his first wife. It was a mystery. No one had ever seen Reverend DoLittle's first wife. They did not know where she was from or where she had gone. Reverend DoLittle had spent his time as the proprietor of the Little Place Pizzeria. His five children moved with his second wife Dorletta May to Louisiana, which was her home. She had never felt comfortable on the shore.

The sisters tried to tempt Reverend DoLittle. He was tall and slender and had graying hair at his temples. He was an exquisite dresser, and now he was single again. He would drive to church in his brand new BMW, dark purple trimmed in gold. He stepped out of his BMW, gave the sisters a smile and a wink, and continued with God's business.

Evangelist Daisy Lou Tarry conducted third Sunday services. She was a widow and the mother of ten adult children. She was a petite woman, and you would never guess she had ten children. She worked out at the local gym doing Pilates and other exercises. She had just written her tenth book—five erotic novels and five books of poetry. Everyone wondered where she got her inspiration. She was such a God-fearing woman. Her message on third Sunday made you think of your life with God. She was always positive in her approach to women's issues.

Reverend Jewel Sugarland was the owner of the local Sugarland's Boutique. Her boutique was one of the most popular in the area. Many of the Mount Grace members shopped there. Her clothes were one of a kind. She dressed to the nines every Sunday morning. Her hat, gloves, shoes, handbag, and suit matched perfectly.

She delivered the fourth Sunday sermon. She encouraged the women to put God first. She said, "What God did for me, He can do for you also." But she never could find her glasses.

The women of the congregation would greet Reverend Sugarland after service to find out what she would have on sale the following week. She would give them coupons to use for a 10 percent discount. She left church in her brand-new, shiny red BMW. The women admired her so. She couldn't understand why. She was just living her life as God wanted her to.

Reverend Mon'e Black was on sick leave. She had fallen in the mall and fractured her right hip. She would be in rehab for months and need a lot of therapy and prayers. Her family members were out of the country in the Peace Corps. Church members took turns helping her with her shopping. Deaconess Clay continued to help her with her cleaning and laundry, and she was improving slowly.

Reverend Black had a minor setback when she had an allergic reaction to some of her medications. She called on Nurse Jayleen Grumble for advice. She was rushed to the ER for treatment but was discharged that same evening. Deaconess Clay remained with her until morning. The congregation continued to pray for her to return to Mount Grace.

Reverend Hatfield continued to gain strength through the prayers of his congregation. A month passed. News came that Major Hatfield was being held as a POW at an unknown location. That's when Reverend Hatfield had his second heart attack. Although it was a minor attack, he was readmitted to the cardiac unit at the hospital. Nurse Grumble continued to monitor his care.

Victoria Fox, the youngest daughter of Lucinda Smith was working in the newsroom when the story broke that Major Johnathan Hatfield had been found. Her prayers were answered. She completed her summer internship and was on her way back to Spellman. She would graduate the following May.

The congregation continued to pray for the Hatfield family, and the ministers continued with their scheduled services.

Sister Weeks and her talented daughter Exxon helped with the weekly revival services while the church was in crisis with Reverend Hatfield in the hospital. Many souls were saved.

CHAPTER 7

Healing

Reverend Hatfield was discharged from the hospital. He was transferred to cardiac rehab for strengthening. After months of prayer, Reverend Hatfield was able to return to church. First Lady Hatfield was right by his side. He was weak but was getting stronger every day. The church continued to fast and pray.

Good news came. Major Johnathan Hatfield was freed and was no longer a POW. He was admitted for a short time to a military hospital after his months of capture. The church and the Hatfields were overjoyed. Their prayers were answered.

Captain Jessie Hatfield returned to his fleet in the Arabian Gulf.

Reverend Hatfield began to preach once a month. First Lady Hatfield would sit in the first pew. She would sing her favorite song and encourage Reverend Hatfield.

Deacon Silky Lion and his family with eight children would lead the praise and worship services. Sister Weeks and her daughter Exxon would join them.

The other preachers continued to preach on alternate Sundays, allowing Reverend Hatfield to continue to gain more strength. Soon he would be in the pulpit every Sunday.

Major Johnathan Hatfield was discharged from the hospital and was able to attend church. The entire church was thrilled. Their prayers had been answered. Major Hatfield attended church every Sunday with his parents. They were so proud.

Three months later, Major Hatfield recovered completely and was deployed. The church family was happy for his recovery but sorry he had to leave. A farewell celebration was held in Major Hatfield's honor.

Reverend Hatfield's health continued to improve. The Pastor's Aid Ministry was preparing a banquet for him. Deaconess Clay, Deaconess Green, Sister Lucinda Smith, and many other women of the church volunteered to help. They wanted this to be the best banquet ever.

First Lady Mattie Hatfield and the ladies of the church were so happy. They made their hair and nail appointments at Rubles Hair Salon. Rubles was owned by Elvira Boston. This was the best and most popular salon in town. Elvira Boston was a personal friend of Sister Lucinda Smith.

Elvira lived in one of the newest high-rises in the city. She was a licensed cosmetologist. This was her passion. She had wanted to do this as a young child. She had opened Rubles several years ago. Her business was booming. She had to hire extra staff. She hired only the best.

Elvira had visited Mount Grace on many occasions. She had special attachments to the church, First Lady Hatfield, and the members. It usually took months to get an appointment at Rubles. Elvira closed her salon for the day to allow all of ladies at Mount Grace to have their nail and hair appointments.

She had her best stylists available for all of them. Some wanted weaves, some wanted braids, and others wanted extensions, curls, or perms. Some wigs needed to be tightened. Whatever the ladies wanted, it was available for them.

When all the women were finished with their nail and hair appointments, they all headed to Sugarland's Boutique for their gowns, shoes, and purses. All of the newest styles were available to the church members who were going to the banquet. Jewel Sugarland made a special call to one of her friends at the Men's Clothiers Shop so the men of the church could be fitted with suits or tuxedoes.

A limousine was sent to the Hatfields' home to take them to the banquet. The banquet was held at the country club. The Hatfield children were able to attend. Major Johnathan Hatfield and Captain Jessie Hatfield were given special leave to attend. Everyone who attended had the best time. They would talk about this for years. Everything was perfect.

First Lady Hatfield was glowing. She was wearing a special gown made especially for her in her favorite color of pink. She had a hat to match. She would never be without a hat. She had had her nails and pedicure done that morning. She was so proud of what the church had done for her and her husband. All of her family was around her. They were getting along in age. She did not know how many good years they had left. She was so grateful for this night. Her prayers again had been answered.

The press had been invited. The banquet was featured on the front page of the local press. The members were interviewed. Pictures of the banquet were featured.

CHAPTER 8

Sister Lucinda Smith

Sister Smith moved to the shore area seven years ago. She was called Smithy by her friends. Sister Smith had married her high school sweetheart Rexall Fox. After marrying, they had moved to Mississippi to help his elderly parents and so he could complete his college education at Old Miss University. This had all been new to Lucinda. She had not been a country girl. She had been used to the suburbs.

She had been happy in the beginning. They had had two beautiful girls, Veronica and Victoria. Her family had kept her busy. She would help her mother-in-law with her daily activities. Her father-in-law had been confined to a wheelchair. She had been glad to help her in-laws.

She would make her girls clothes. They would dress like twins. They had been a year apart. They had been the best of friends. Where you had seen one, you would see the other. When the girls had been five, they had been enrolled in school.

Lucinda had found a part-time job in the local library. She had enjoyed reading. This had been the perfect job for her. God had led her to a church she had felt comfortable in called New Star Baptist Church. She and the girls had gone every Sunday. On some Sundays her husband, Rexall, had attended with them.

The girls had been in Sunday school and in the children's choir. They had enjoyed the services. Lucinda had become the church clerk. She would read notices and record information for new members.

Sister Lucinda had prayed to God for guidance and answers. Her marriage to Rexall had become intolerable. He had been more physically and verbally abusive lately. This marriage had not been made by God.

After seven years, Lucinda could not take it anymore. God had given her the answer one night. Leave. Sister Lucinda had not wanted to disrupt her family, but she had had to obey God for her and her daughters' safety. One cold wintery morning, Sister Lucinda had packed up the girls and had caught the first Greyhound bus to New Jersey.

Times had been difficult in the beginning, but with God, they had made it. She had found a small apartment for her and the girls. They had searched for a church home. They had been led to Mount Grace. About five years later, word had been sent to Lucinda that her ex-husband had been killed by his lover's husband. She had had to break the news to her teenage daughters. They had taken the news hard.

Lucinda met Jaylee Grumble at the library. They became instant friends. They were from similar backgrounds and had the same interests. Jaylee was divorced and a mother of three boys. She was head nurse at the hospital in the ICU unit. She loved God. She enjoyed traveling. Her sons and Lucinda's daughters got along well. They had vacationed together when the children were younger. The families had gone on an African safari when the children had been teenagers. They had enjoyed cruising on the Royal Caribbean Line.

Five years later, Lucinda fell in love. It was a marriage that was blessed by God. She married Jerry Smith. Jerry was a New Jersey Transit bus driver. They bought a lovely home in town for their family. Lucinda completed her college education in hospital administration. She was made administrator of the local nursing home.

Jerry Smith was the eldest of five children. His father had died when he was a young child. He had helped his mother raise his two brothers and two sisters. Jerry had had little time for himself.

He was glad the day he met Lucinda and her girls. Now he had a family of his own he could devote his time to. Jerry would take them to car races and sporting events, which the girls loved. The girls adored Jerry. After they bought their home, they went on road trips together as a family. Jerry loved to drive. Jerry adored Lucinda. He was so proud of her accomplishments. Jerry would always brag to his friends about his wife and what she had done.

Lucinda was glad she was able to supervise her mother's care. She had to admit her mother into a nursing home. Her mother had sold their family home after the death of her husband. She had bought a small ranch house in a retirement village. Her mother was ninety. She suffered from dementia, She fell frequently.

After her mother fractured her hip, Lucinda continued to worry about her mother's safety. She had a nurse come to her home to care for her. Her condition deteriorated. Finally, she had put her mother in the nursing home. Her mother would receive the best of care there. Lucinda called on her best nursing assistants, Cassie and Vonda, for help. They loved her mother. She was like a grandmother to them. This was the best choice Lucinda could make.

Mr. Henry Keele was her understanding boss. He owned two nursing homes in the area. He always approved her vacation time. She planned her vacation with her girls, her friend Jaylee, and Jaylee's boys. They cruised the Caribbean.

They sailed to the Virgin Islands. Lucinda's husband did not like to travel. He had no problem with Lucinda traveling with her friend Jayleen.

On many cruises, Lucinda's younger sister Millie would join them. Lucinda's parents had had Millie when they were older. Lucinda had taken care of Millie. She had gotten her ready for school, had combed her hair, had made sure she was dressed appropriately, and had taught her to tie her shoes.

Lucinda adored her little sister. Millie had looked to Lucinda for guidance when she was young. She had been happy to be in her presence. Now, Lucinda would ask her sister Millie for advice. Millie had grown in knowledge. Lucinda found her advice useful. Millie would give Lucinda advice on her past experiences. The roles seemed to have reversed. Millie was always happy to travel with Lucinda and Jayleen.

Lucinda's sister Rosie married young. She had a husband and four children. She did not have the time or money to travel with her sisters. She was happy for them. When her children were older, she planned to join them on their cruises. She enjoyed receiving the postcards and the e-mails they sent from the many new and exciting destinations.

Someone always wanted to travel with Lucinda and the group. Lucinda's two nieces, Kesha and Katie, traveled with them when they were able to take vacation time.

Kesha Berry was a single mother of four. She was manager in the furniture department of a local department store called Flowers. She had worked at the store for ten years and was now manager. Her children were so proud of her. She was dedicated to Flowers.

Katie Brown was married and a mother of three girls. Katie was director of customer accounts at the electric company. Katie juggled her time between church, family, and her job. Katie and her husband Ken loved to travel. When she was not traveling with Ken, she traveled with her aunt Lucinda.

Lucinda and her girls continued to work in the church. She became an usher and a church notary. Reverend Hatfield offered her the position of church clerk and then financial secretary. Lucinda was always good at balancing her checkbook. She had great respect for Reverend Hatfield, so she gladly accepted the position. She enjoyed helping out with the Pastor's Aid Ministry (PAM), Vacation Bible School, and Easter and Christmas pageants.

Deaconess Clay was president of the PAM. She asked Lucinda if she would like to help. Of course, Lucinda said yes. They were working on the banquet. It was such a great success. They worked well together. They worked on many church functions together.

CHAPTER 9

Changes

There had been many changes at Mount Grace. Reverend DoLittle had been seeing former debutante socialite Mary Jane Barrington. Mary Jane Barrington was the daughter of prominent attorney Carl Barrington. After college graduation, her parents sent her to Europe with several of her friends. She had just returned from some exotic place.

She was their only child. She was always jetting off somewhere with her friends. The crowd she traveled with enjoyed what she enjoyed. Her parents felt that now that she was twenty-eight, it was time for her to take life more seriously and to settle down.

Her parents bought her a nail salon called Just Nails. They hoped this would give her some stability. She hired a full staff. She was at the salon occasionally. On one of these occasions, she met Reverend Timothy DoLittle. He was there for a manicure. She caught his eye. They started seeing each other. She was twenty years his junior. They did not seem to have a problem with their age difference. They were in love. She introduced him to her parents. Her parents were not sure about the age difference.

ReverendTimothy DoLittle introduced Mary Jane to the members at Mount Grace. They were happy for him. They only wanted the best for Reverend DoLittle. They prayed he had found the right wife this time.

One year later, they married. They had a large wedding at the country club. The entire church was invited. All of the Barringtons' friends were there.

Deaconess Clara Clay's husband died suddenly after injuries he had received in an auto accident. Deaconess Clay was devastated that he had been taken so soon. The church prayed for her to find peace. She was hospitalized several times. She never fully recovered from her husband's death. Her family tried to console her. Her church family tried to console her.

Deaconess Clay resigned from the Pastor's Aid Ministry (PAM). She moved to California with her sister. Mount Grace was sad to see her go. They continued to pray for her.

Deaconess Jean Green felt lost without her sister in Christ. It was difficult to work without her. She prayed for strength.

Deaconess Green was having trouble in her marriage. Six months after Deaconess Clay moved, Deaconess Green's husband left her for a younger woman he had been seeing. She was thirty years his junior.

Deaconess Green felt hurt and devastated. She looked for answers. Why did this happen to her? She immersed herself in work at the church. She took on more responsibilities to fill her time. She eventually resigned as a PAM member. It was too hard to work without her friend, Deaconess Clay.

Sister Lucinda Smith's girls were now in college. Veronica was at Delaware State University. Her major was political science. Victoria was at Spellman College in Atlanta, Georgia, majoring in journalism. They were doing well. Sister Lucinda continued to work in the church, helping wherever she was needed.

Her friend Jayleen's sons were also at college. Charles was at Howard University in Washington DC. Kerry was at Princeton University in New Jersey. Julian was at Columbia University in New York City.

They missed their children. They thanked God their children were healthy and doing well. They would spend more time at church. Then they would take cruise together. They discussed a cruise fundraising idea with the church. Some members were receptive, and some were not. The idea never got off the ground.

Sister Martha Sitter had retired recently as the head receptionist at a chiropractor's office, Dr. Backs. She was the church's clerk. She had devoted her life to God, her church, her younger daughter Amanda, and her only grandson Joshua. They enjoyed long walks on the beach, shopping at Walmart, and going to church together.

On one of their trips to the super Walmart, Amanda had met Matthew. Martha was pleased. She liked Matthew. He would be good for Amanda. Amanda was shy, and Matthew was outgoing.

Sister Amanda Sitter became engaged to Matthew Righthand after six months. They had a whirlwind love affair. They continued to shop at the super Walmart. This was their little private joke.

They were two people who deserved the love God had blessed them with. They had a large, beautiful wedding at Mount Grace. The pastor gave them his blessing. The whole church attended. They flew to Aruba for a two-week honeymoon.

Head usher, Sister Missy Starr was trying to recruit new members for the usher board. She had been the head usher for the past five years. She had a difficult job. She enjoyed her position. She enjoyed being in control. She was in the process trying to start a junior usher unit with the young children that were in the choir.

Trustee Phillips was promoted to head supervisor at Wonderland, the local amusement park. He was a dedicated employee. He was rewarded for his twenty years of service. He was given a special cart to ride in as he checked the grounds of the park. It was so well deserved. Trustee Phillips would give the families with children discount tickets to Wonderland. He was loyal to Reverend DoLittle.

Sister Exxon Weeks, daughter of Sister Weeks, led morning devotions and was in charge of the praise team. She had just received a four-year scholarship to the Conservatory of Music in Philadelphia. She had the voice of an angel. She would be missed. Sister Soledade Lions, wife of Deacon Silky Lions, would take over her duties gladly.

The Lions family was fairly new to Mount Grace. When they were not in church, you could find them in their minivan spreading the gospel in the community and feeding the homeless. They enjoyed giving.

Danny Lax was the church drummer. He had just turned eighteen. Danny would be graduating from high school that summer. He was one of the young men Major Johnathan Hatfield had mentored when he was in town. Danny had decided to enlist in the marines. Major Hatfield was his idol. His parents were thrilled he was on the right path.

Joshua Glee played the piano for the church. Joshua was in his late twenties. He was the only grandson of Sister Martha Sitter. He was an accomplished musician. Joshua and his finance Joy would sing and travel together. Joy just completed a tour with the Metropolitan Opera. They were recently featured on the new TV show *The New Voice*. Joy had an incredible voice. She sang some Sundays with Exxon Weeks.

Joshua was offered a recording contract with his finance Joy. They would be going to Hollywood to fulfill their dreams in the near future.

Sister Mary Jane DoLittle, wife of Reverend Timothy DoLittle, gave birth to their first child, a son. He was eight pounds and twenty-two inches. They named their son Timothy Jr. after his father. Her parents were overjoyed. This was their first grandchild.

New Mount Grace member, Sister Racheal Bright, was a wife, mother of triplet boys, and grandmother of two beautiful boys. Sister Bright was the dean of a local university. She spent long hours helping students with their career choices. She was dedicated to her students. She was a God-fearing woman.

Her husband was a leading architect and played the piano at churches in the area. Her husband Barry's work could be seen along the shore. His work was exquisite. His buildings were made of glass with a cross on the top, as to say God has blessed this building. The buildings are usually by the ocean.

Two of Sister Bright's sons, Matthew and Mark, graduated from law school and opened their law firm in town. Her third son, Julius, graduated from Monmouth University. He taught biology at the high school. He married his childhood sweetheart Ruth the year before that. His wife was a teacher at the high school also. They had twin sons named James and John.

Reverend Hatfield had been in guarded health for the past several months. This had happened after his banquet. Sister Hatfield was worried. She prayed for his health and the strength to see her through. She asked the church to continue to pray for her family. Reverend Hatfield had just turned eighty. Then Reverend Hatfield was rushed to the hospital with severe chest pains. The congregation continued to pray for the pastor ...

CHAPTER 10

Death of the Pastor

Reverend Hatfield continued to have episodes of chest pain. He was taken back to ICU.

Sister Hatfield remained by his side. Reverend Justice Ritz and Reverend Jewel Sugarland took turns praying and sitting with Sister Hatfield. The stress had taken a toll on her. Her children all flew in to be with their parents at this difficult time.

The church set up a prayer vigil. They prayed day and night.

Reverend Hatfield sent for Reverend DoLittle, asking him to come to the hospital. Reverend Hatfield wanted Reverend DoLittle to take care of his church and his people if he was called home. Reverend DoLittle made a promise to Reverend Hatfield that he would be obedient.

One week later, Reverend Hatfield closed his eyes and went home to be with the Lord. Sister Mattie Hatfield never left her husband's side. She felt so alone. They had been married for over fifty years. What was she to do? He had done everything for her. She prayed to God for guidance and peace. Her children and the church members rallied around her. The church felt at a great loss. Reverend Hatfield had been their pastor for over forty years.

Victoria Fox had graduated from Spellman College. She worked as a junior reporter at a local paper in Atlanta. She asked for the assignment to cover the funeral of her beloved pastor, Reverend Hatfield. She flew to New Jersey to cover the story for Atlanta. She saw her friend Jon and his family. She gave her condolences. She covered the passing of Reverend Hatfield. The story made all the papers.

The church prepared for the funeral of this great man and pastor. Dignitaries from all states were notified. Word spread fast of this great loss. Telegrams were received from fifty states. Proclamations were sent from the governors. A special letter of condolence was sent by the president of the United States.

Flags were flown at half-mast for thirty days. The military sent special guards the day of the funeral. Mount Grace was so full, there was standing room only. The entire town came out to pay its respects. The streets were lined with mourners. The schools were closed. The press covered the services. This was a fitting send-off for such a humble man of God.

The mass choirs, from many churches in the state, attended. The police and fire departments, the hospital's staff, and so many more attended.

Head usher, Sister Missy Starr, was busy with her staff, trying to seat everyone before the service started. Ushers from area churches were assisting her.

Many preachers and ministers spoke. Limits had to be placed on their time because there were so many. The service lasted for hours. Everyone wanted to participate

Many ministers wanted to give the eulogy. Sister Hatfield chose Reverend Hatfield's longtime friend, Reverend Maxwell. He gave a touching eulogy of the man he had known and loved as his friend.

Sister Hatfield remained in mourning for one year. She felt so lost. She continued to pray to God. Her children and grandchildren were a great help to her. The church members kept her in prayer. They would sit and pray with her after all of her children returned to their respective homes.

The high school was named after him—John Hatfield High School. Streets and places were named after him—Hatfield

Boulevard, Hatfield Library, Hatfield Fire Department. The list went on and on.

A special meeting was called to make it official. The members voted to make Reverend DoLittle the new pastor of Mount Grace Church. Reverend Timothy DoLittle was now the pastor of Mount Grace. Reverend. Justice Ritz would be his right-hand man.

All other officers would remain in their positions. They were in need of a new Pastor's Aid Ministry (PAM) president because Deaconess Clay had left.

Sister Donna Miller was asked to fill the position. Sister Miller was perfect for the position. She was well liked by the church members, and she loved the Lord. Sister Miller worked tirelessly as president. She chaired many functions. She was a great fundraiser. She organized the praise team to help the PAM reach young members. Sister Miller took ill suddenly and passed away soon after this. The members were in shock. They still needed a PAM president.

Sister Racheal Bright was offered the position and gladly accepted. This would be challenging for her because she was a new member under new leadership. Sister Racheal Bright felt she was up for the task.

She tried to organize her staff, but members were dedicated to the former ministry. They had to make adjustments. This would be a slow process. She prayed to God for help. Sister Lucinda Smith was glad to offer her help. Sister Bright gladly accepted it. Some members left, but new members came.

CHAPTER 11

Victoria Fox was now a leading reporter at the newspaper in Atlanta. She had just flown in to interview Sister Nora Lane for a story she was doing about Sister Lane's humanitarian efforts in Soweto, South Africa, and Labadee, Haiti. Sister Lane had been Victoria's Sunday school teacher when she had attended Mount Grace as a child. The story made national headlines: "Local Former Kindergarten and Sunday School Teacher Becomes Superintendent and Continues to Help Children."

Sister Mary Jane DoLittle gave birth to their second child, a little girl they named Lucy. She weighed 9 pounds and was nineteen inches long. She was the image of her mother. Her grandmother doted on her.

As little Lucy grew, her grandmother took her to Broadway plays, the opera, and the ballet. She spent as much time as possible with little Lucy. She felt her life was complete. She had a granddaughter.

Reverend Timothy was now in his new position. He wanted to be addressed as Pastor DoLittle. There were many changes under the new administration. He was busy with his new family and his new position at Mount Grace.

The Pastor's Aid Ministry helped the pastor and the church. New members joined.

The pastor had a new armor-bearer, Sister Alice Ready. She enjoyed helping the pastor. Sister Ready was a retired English teacher. She had a lot of free time. She would sometimes go to the movies with her friend Sister Missy Starr. They went to Bible study together. She volunteered at the soup kitchen and the library. She lived alone. She did not have family in the area. She devoted many hours to the church. She enjoyed helping with the Sunday school.

Sister Lucinda Smith decided it was time to take another cruise. There had been so many changes recently. She cruised the Bahamas with her brother Devin, her sister Millie, and Rosie. This was her brother's first cruise. She had cruised many times with her sister. She was planning her next cruise to Asia with her friend Jayleen and her sister Millie. This was a way for her to relax. God continued to bless Lucinda.

The Pastor's Aid Ministry planned a church picnic. Sister Hatfield offered her home as she had done when Reverend Hatfield had been alive. Out of respect for the late Reverend Hatfield, the church gathered to give support to Sister Hatfield. Everyone tried to enjoy the picnic. They kept Reverend Hatfield in the back of their minds.

It had been five years since the passing of Reverend Hatfield. The DoLittle children were getting older. They were involved in more activities—baseball games, cheerleading, piano lessons, ballet, and drums—which required their parents' participation. They were constantly on the go with their growing family. They attended PTA meetings and went on school trips.

Sister DoLittle rarely visited her nail salon. She just did not have the time. She hired a full-time manager.

Pastor DoLittle experienced the same situation. He was pastor of the church and was involved in his young children's activities. You could see the stress he was now under. He was rarely at the pizzeria. Reverend Ritz and Reverend Sugarland would deliver the sermon some Sunday morning.

The ministerial staff tried to help the pastor as much possible. The pastor started to have migraine headaches. His doctor thought the stress contributed to this. He had to slow down.

Pastor DoLittle was also appointed director of Helping Hands. This department helped children at risk.

Pastor DoLittle was also planning to build a new church for the growing congregation. The church needed a day care for the growing number of children. They needed an educational center for the adult classes. They were running out of space. There was so much to be done.

Pastor DoLittle planned for the next annual church picnic to be held at his modest home. Would all the members be able to fit inside? His space was very limited.

His mother-in-law, Gigi Barrington, invited all of their friends. After all, this was her daughter's home also. Her grandchildren would be there, she adored them. She enjoyed her time with them.

Pastor DoLittle was experiencing headaches more frequently. His fingers felt numb at times. Nurse Grumble spoke to the pastor to find out when he had had his last physical. She encouraged him to make an appointment with his family doctor.

CHAPTER 12

Where is Pastor DoLillle?

The church service was just beginning on that Sunday morning. There was a light dusting of snow on the ground. Members were very slowly ushered in by the head usher Sister Missy Starr. She was always at her post. Had Sister Lucinda Smith remembered to do the mass call to let the members know the service would start later due to the weather?

The praise and worship team of ten people were singing their hearts out. Sister Exxon was singing a solo. Mother Hatfield joined in with her favorite song—whatever her favorite song of the day was.

Everyone was getting into the service, when all of a sudden, there was a loud, thunderous crash! The entire choir platform with all of the musicians and the equipment crashed into the basement. Everyone was yelling and praying. They asked, "Where is the pastor? Where is our shepherd? Is anyone hurt? Trustees, call 911. There may be spinal injuries."

The musicians were taken to the ER. Head nurse Jayleen Grumble came down from ICU when she heard what had happened. Danny and Joshua were glad to see a familiar face.

Danny had a fractured right leg. Joshua had fractured his left arm. Danny and Joshua had multiple abrasions and bruises. The injuries were not life threatening. They were taken into surgery to have the fractures set.

Joshua's injury would affect his playing the piano for several weeks. They were both admitted overnight. Nurse Grumble made sure they had a room together and the best of care. They were discharged to go home the following afternoon. They would not be able to play at the church for several weeks. The church continued to pray for their recovery.

The church prayed that God would send them two musicians who could fill in for Danny and Joshua. They were sent Thomas and Jackson. Their father, Reverend Goode, was the pastor from a neighboring church. He was also a friend of Pastor DoLittle. He was glad to help. They were glad to be of service. There was music again in the church. God had answered their prayers.

There was still no sign of Pastor DoLittle. Pastor DoLittle had been under stress for several months. Pastor was always in the pulpit by 11 a.m., but no one had seen him that morning. The trustees called his home. There was no answer. Maybe he had been running late. They decided to wait ten more minutes.

CHAPTER 13

Foul Play?

Trustee Matthew Righthand and Trustee Daniel Phillips made a trip to Pastor DoLittle's home. No one was home. They found that strange. Then they remembered. Young Tim Jr. had a baseball game today. The trustees went to the ball field. Tim was pitching, and his sister Lucy was cheering.

The trustees spoke with Sister Mary Jane DoLittle, asking about the pastor. She thought he had gone to church. She had not seen him since the night before. He had been fasting and praying. They decided to wait a few hours to see if showed up. Sister DoLittle did not seem concerned at the time. She continued to enjoy the game.

The next day, the trustees called Sister DoLittle. She had not seen the pastor. Now she was very concerned. Where was her husband? Where was the pastor? There was no sign of Pastor DoLittle. The trustees decided to check the pizzeria the pastor owned. The trustees spoke with the employees. No one had seen the pastor. They checked his office and his private bathroom at the pizzeria. On the sink, they saw what appeared to be fresh blood.

They decided to call the police. The police told them not to touch anything. The police spoke with all of the employees. No one had seen Pastor DoLittle since Friday afternoon.

The police called their CSI unit. The CSI unit arrived. They interviewed all the employees. They took fingerprints and a sample of the blood found on the sink for DNA. The sample tested positive as being from Pastor DoLittle, but there was no sign of a struggle.

Word reached the church and the community. The story had broken when Victoria Fox was in New Jersey celebrating with her family. She had just received the Pulitzer Prize for journalism on the story she did about Superintendent Nora Lane. She had since moved to Tampa Bay, Florida, to be close to her sister, Veronica.

Veronica had graduated from law school. She was a practicing attorney in Tampa Bay for civil rights and immigration. On every third Saturday, Veronica held a seminar on domestic violence, an issue she passionate about. She had firsthand experience with domestic violence from a former boyfriend during law school. Veronica's passion was to give information to all women or men in an abusive relationship. Her door was always open.

Veronica and Victoria had enjoyed the shoreline when they were growing up in New Jersey. It was the perfect location for them.

Victoria Fox was now a reporter, she started doing some investigating on her own. Earlier Victoria Fox was in print journalism. She was not sure if she enjoyed writing the news stories or reporting the news. She was now the six o'clock anchor at a local television station. She knew the family well. She made an appeal on the six o'clock news, asking the community to help in the search for Pastor DoLittle. A toll-free number was provided for any information.

Pastor DoLittle was missing. Was it because of foul play? Where was Pastor DoLittle? They dragged the lake near his home. No evidence was found. All of his employees were fingerprinted. Sister DoLittle was questioned again. The children were crying for their father. His in-laws, the Barringtons, were questioned. No one had seen him in the past week. Where was the pastor? The church continued to pray.

The FBI was called in. Was the pastor on the way to the bank to deposit the tithes and offerings from last week's service? He would sometimes do this when Sister Smith was on vacation. Sister Lucinda Smith was on vacation in Florida with her sisters and unaware of what was happening in New Jersey. Was there a robbery? The bank verified that all deposits had been made.

It was now the end of the second week. The pastor was still missing. Reverend Ritz and Reverend Sugarland had been delivering sermons in the absence of their pastor. Evangelist Daisy Lou Tarry was notified. She was unable to help. She was on her fifth book tour, promoting her latest book. She would pray that the pastor would be found safe.

CHAPTER 14

Found

The Royal Caribbean Anthem of the Seas was just pulling into St. Maarten's Port. The Anthem was one of the newest ships in the line. She was beautiful. All of the newest technologies were featured on this ship, which was on a seven port-of-call cruise. The water was a royal blue color. The scenery was beautiful. There were three other cruise ships docked there.

The passengers were disembarking. They were posing for pictures. Some passengers went shopping, some took tours, and some remained on deck relaxing.

Sitting by the pool with his Bible in his hand was Pastor DoLittle, relaxing. Pastor DoLittle had stopped by the Little Place Pizzeria late on Saturday to check supplies. The supplies had been fully stocked. He had stopped in his office to do some paperwork and then gone in the private bathroom to shave. He had accidently nicked himself while shaving. He had left through the private entrance.

He had taken an Uber ride to Cape Liberty in Bayonne, New Jersey, early Sunday morning and boarded the Anthem for a two-week eastern Caribbean cruise.

This was his first cruise. Sister Smith had been right. This cruise was so relaxing. His headaches were gone. He felt stronger and more relaxed. This was something he really needed. God knew what he needed. He would plan another cruise when he returned home and he would take his family. Had he remembered to call Sister Smith to have her let the church members and his family know he would be away for two weeks on a Caribbean cruise?

Sunday morning, the church service had already begun when Pastor DoLittle arrived. He was unaware that everyone thought he was missing. Pastor DoLittle explained what had happened and where he had been the past two weeks.

Mount Grace members were all relieved the pastor was safe. They thanked God for the safe return of their pastor and shepherd. Their prayers had been answered.

Mount Grace continues to grow. The church's expansion will begin in the near future.

Printed in the United States
By Bookmasters